Atsuko Morozumi

FOR VINCENT AND RICHARD

This edition first published in the UK 2004
©1977 Atsuko Morozumi
Designed by Douglas Martin
Produced by Mathew Price Ltd
The Old Glove Factory, Bristol Road
Sherborne, Dorset DT9 4HP
Printed in China

My Friend Gorilla

MATHEW PRICE LIMITED

When they closed the zoo, my Daddy
brought home a gorilla.

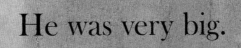
He was very big.

But he was friendly.

And very helpful.

I liked him.

And he liked me.

My Daddy said that he could
stay with us for a while.

He was my friend.

He came to my birthday party.

He stayed through the Autumn.

Then one day some people came.
They said my gorilla used to live in Africa,
and he would be happier there.

They said they would come back another day
to take him home.

It was a snowy day when my gorilla left.

One day a letter came from Africa.

In it was a photograph of my gorilla.
He looked happy, and I felt happy too.

I still remember him.